GK

THE *Christmas* SECRET

*Will an 1880 Christmas Eve wedding
be cancelled by revelations in an old diary?*

THE
Christmas
SECRET

Wanda E. Brunstetter

SHILOH RUN PRESS
An Imprint of Barbour Publishing, Inc.

© 2011 by Wanda E. Brunstetter

Print ISBN 978-1-63409-675-1

eBook Editions:
Adobe Digital Edition (.epub) 978-1-68322-030-5
Kindle and MobiPocket Edition (.prc) 978-1-68322-031-2

All scripture quotations are taken from the King James Version of the Bible.

This book is a work of fiction. Names, characters, places, and incidents are either products of the author's imagination or used fictitiously. Any similarity to actual people, organizations, and/or events is purely coincidental.

Cover design: Buffy Cooper
Cover model photography: Richard Brunstetter III; RBIII Studios

Published by Shiloh Run Press, a division of Barbour Publishing, Inc., P.O. Box 719, Uhrichsville, Ohio 44683, www.barbourbooks.com

Our mission is to publish and distribute inspirational products offering exceptional value and biblical encouragement to the masses.

ECPA Member of the
Evangelical Christian
Publishers Association

Printed in Canada.

Dedication

To Phil and Diane Allen, our special Pennsylvania friends.
Thanks for all you do.

Trust in the LORD with all thine heart;
and lean not unto thine own understanding.

PROVERBS 3:5

Chapter 1

*F*eeling the need for a bit of fresh air, Elizabeth Canning opened her bedroom window and drew in a deep breath, inhaling the earthy, leaf-scented fragrance that she knew even with her eyes closed was like no other season but autumn.

When a chilling wind blew in, rustling the lace curtains and causing her to shiver, she quickly shut the window. It was too cold for the first of November. Did the nippy weather mean they were in for a harsh winter this year, or would they be spared and have only a few bitterly cold days? Whatever the case, she hoped they'd have snow for Christmas. God's sparkling white crystals always added a little something extra to the beauty and atmosphere of the holiday season.

Through the closed window, Elizabeth heard geese honking in the distance, no doubt making their southward journey. She could almost feel their excitement as they flew to warmer territories. It never failed, spring or fall; hearing geese high in the sky stirred a thrill deep in her soul.

When a knock sounded on the door, Elizabeth turned and called, "Come in."

The door opened, and Elizabeth's friend, Helen Warner, entered the room. Her coal-black hair, worn in a chignon at the back of her head and covered with a silver net, stood in sharp

contrast to Elizabeth's golden-blond hair, which she wore hanging loosely down her back today. But then, Helen, who'd recently turned twenty, had always been the prim and proper one, often wearing high-neck dresses with perfectly shaped bustles, like the one she wore today. Elizabeth, on the other hand, was the practical type and preferred full-skirted calico dresses, which were more comfortable when one was cleaning or working around the house. She felt rather plain next to Helen, but fortunately their friendship was based on more than the clothes they wore or their differing opinions on some things.

Elizabeth's meticulous friend was outgoing and always seemed to have an air of excitement about her. Maybe Helen's confident demeanor came from being the daughter of an esteemed minister of the largest congregation in Allentown, for she had a certain charisma that glowed like a halo around her. To Elizabeth, it was most invigorating, even though she, herself, was more down-to-earth.

"I thought you were going to help me clean the cabin today,

but it doesn't look like you came dressed for work," Elizabeth said.

"I was hoping you'd change your mind and go shopping with me instead." When Helen took a seat on the feather bed, her long, purple stockings peeked out from under the hem of her matching dress.

Elizabeth's brows furrowed. "There's no time for shopping right now. If David and I are to be married on Christmas Eve, then it doesn't give us much time to get the cabin cleaned and ready for the wedding."

Helen's brown eyes narrowed, causing tiny wrinkles to form across her forehead. "It's one thing to have the ceremony in the cabin, since you're only inviting family and close friends, but are you sure you want to live in that dreary little place? It's so small, and far from town."

"It's not that far—only a few miles." Elizabeth took a seat beside her friend. "The cabin has special meaning to me. It was the first home of my mother's parents, and soon after Grandma

and Grandpa moved to Easton, Mother married Daddy, and they moved into the cabin to begin their life together. They lived there until. . ." Elizabeth's voice trailed off, and she blinked to hold back tears threatening to spill over. "After Mother died of pneumonia when I was eight years old, Daddy couldn't stand to live there any longer, because everything in the cabin reminded him of her." Elizabeth may have been young, but she remembered how empty and lifeless the cabin had felt once her mother was gone.

"So you moved to town and lived at the Main Street Boardinghouse, right?"

Elizabeth nodded. "We stayed there until I was ten, and then when Daddy got his shoemaking business going well and married Abigail, we moved into the house he had built." She smiled and touched Helen's arm. "Soon after that, I met you."

"So you're used to living in town now, and just because your parents and grandparents lived in the cabin doesn't mean you have to."

"David and I want to begin our life together there." Elizabeth

sighed. "Besides, he's just getting started with his carriage-making business and can't afford to have a home built for us here right now."

"I understand that, but can't you continue living with your father and stepmother or even at the hotel David's grandfather owns?"

"I suppose we could, but it wouldn't be the same as having a place of our own to call home."

Helen folded her arms with an undignified grunt. "Humph! That cabin isn't a home; it's a hovel. If David's so poor that he can't offer you more, then maybe you should consider marrying someone else. Maybe someone like Howard Glenstone. I think he's been interested in you for some time."

"I'm not in love with Howard. I love David, and I'd be happy living in the cabin with him for the rest of my life if necessary." It was obvious to Elizabeth that Helen didn't understand or appreciate how the homey little dwelling came to be. It must have taken a lot of hard work, frustration, and long hours for her

mother's father to build the cabin for Grandma and the family they'd one day have. How proud Grandpa must have been, knowing he'd built the place with his own two hands.

"I just think a woman as beautiful as you could do much better," Helen said.

Elizabeth bristled. "Are you saying that David's not an attractive man?"

Helen placed her hand on Elizabeth's arm. "I'm not saying that at all. David has very nice features, and with both of you having golden-blond hair and vivid blue eyes, you make a striking couple." She patted the sides of her hair. "Of course, I'd never be attracted to anyone who had the same color hair and eyes as me."

"When you meet the right man and fall in love, you won't care what color his hair and eyes are, because real love isn't based on a person's looks." Elizabeth touched her chest. "It's what's in the heart that counts. While I do think David is quite handsome, the things that drew me to him were his kind, gentle spirit and the fact that he's a fine Christian man."

"He does seem to be all that." Helen smiled at Elizabeth. "I'm sure the two of you will have sweet, even-tempered children with beautiful blond hair and pretty blue eyes."

Elizabeth smiled. "I'm looking forward to becoming a mother. In fact, I'm looking forward to every aspect of being married."

"Including cooking and cleaning?" Helen's nose wrinkled.

"Yes, even that." The springs in the bed squeaked as Elizabeth rose to her feet. "Speaking of cleaning, I should hitch my horse to the buckboard so we can go over to the cabin now."

Helen gestured to her fancy dress. "I suppose I should change into one of your calicos first."

Elizabeth pointed to her wardrobe across the room. "Feel free to wear whichever one you want."

❄

David Stinner had never been one to shirk his duties, but today he was having a hard time staying focused on his work. All he could think about was Elizabeth, and how he couldn't wait to make her his wife. They'd been courting nearly a year and would

be married on Christmas Eve. He couldn't think of any better Christmas present for himself than making Elizabeth his bride, and she insisted that getting married to him on her birthday was the best gift she could receive for turning twenty. She was everything he wanted in a wife—sweet-tempered, patient, intelligent, beautiful, and a Christian in every sense of the word. She would make not only a good wife but also a fine mother to the children they might have someday.

"Hey, boss, how come you've been standin' there holdin' that piece of wood for so long?"

David whirled around, surprised to see his helper, Gus Smith, standing behind him. When he'd last seen Gus, he'd been at the back of the shop, cutting a stack of wood.

"I wish you wouldn't sneak up on me like that," David said, shaking his head. "I nearly dropped this piece of oak for the sideboards of Arnold Higgin's bakery wagon."

Gus's bushy dark eyebrows lifted high on his forehead. "Looked to me like you were just standin' there holdin' that piece

of wood, and you're nowhere near the body of the bakery wagon you started yesterday."

"I was taking a few minutes to think, that's all."

"Thinkin' about your bride-to-be, I'll bet."

David nodded, his face heating with embarrassment. He hated how easily he blushed.

"Are ya gettin' cold feet?"

"Of course not. I was just thinking about how Elizabeth and her friend, Helen, are going to the cabin to do some cleaning today. I wish I could be there to help them."

"Why can't ya be?"

David glanced across the room, noting the bakery wagon he'd been about to work on. Then there was an emerald-green carriage needing a new set of wheels, a coal-box buggy that was only half built, and the town coach the banker had brought in yesterday for new axles and springs. "I have too much work to do here right now. I promised to have the bakery wagon done by the end of next week, not to mention the other orders we have waiting." Some days could be a bit overwhelming, but David was grateful for the work and good relationships he'd been building with his customers. He was also humbled by their trust in the fine craftsman he was proving himself to be.

"Maybe you can go over to the cabin when you're done workin' today," Gus suggested.

"That's what I'm hoping to do." David leaned the piece of wood against the wall.

Gus moved closer to David. "You still gonna live in the log cabin after you and Elizabeth are married?"

David nodded.

"Wouldn't ya rather live at the hotel your granddaddy owns? It'd be closer to your shop and has a lot more conveniences than the cabin."

"It wouldn't be our own place, and all we'd have is one small room."

"That dinky old cabin ain't much bigger than a hotel room." Gus snorted like an old bull.

"It's big enough for our needs, and once my business grows, I can either add on to the cabin or have a house built for us here in town."

Just then, David's mother rushed into the shop, wearing no shawl around her shoulders, despite the chilly day. "Come quickly, David! Your grandfather fell from a ladder, and he doesn't respond!" Her hazel-colored eyes were wide with fear, and a lock of reddish-brown hair had come loose from the chignon at the back of her head. David figured she must have run all the way here.

"I'll be back as soon as I can," David called to Gus. He grabbed his mother's hand, and they rushed out the door.

Chapter 2

When David and his mother entered the hotel foyer, he was surprised to see his grandfather standing behind the front desk, where the hotel guests were greeted. He appeared to be unhurt. Had Mother made the whole thing up just to get him to come over here? If so, what was the reason? He was about to ask when Mother swooped across the room and rushed to Grandpa's side.

"Papa, are you okay?" She clutched his arm so tightly that

David wondered if she would bruise the old man's skin.

After Grandma died of pneumonia three years ago, Mother had been overprotective of Grandpa. Then when David's father was killed a year later in an accident at the steel mill, she'd almost smothered Grandpa to death.

"I'm fine, Carolyn," Grandpa said, pushing her hand away. "Just had the wind knocked out of me when I fell. If you hadn't rushed out of here so quickly, I'd have told you that."

"But you weren't responding to anything I said. You were lying on the floor with your eyes closed. That's why I went to get David." She took a deep breath and closed her eyes—no doubt in an effort to calm herself.

Grandpa's gaze shifted to David, who had moved to stand beside his mother. "Were you working at the carriage shop?" he questioned.

David nodded.

"I'm sorry she bothered you for nothing." Grandpa looked at Mother and then back at David. "You know how emotional your

mother can be. She probably thought I was dead."

"That's exactly what I thought," Mother said with a catch in her voice.

"Grandpa, what were you doing on the ladder?" David asked.

"I was trying to straighten that." Grandpa motioned to the slightly crooked oil painting hanging above an enormous stone fireplace on the other side of the room. One of the local artists had painted the picture of the hotel soon after it had opened for business nearly thirty years ago.

Mother pursed her lips. "You should have waited for our handyman to do it, Papa."

"Seth's out running an errand right now."

"I realize that, but I'm sure he'll be back soon, and you really should have waited."

Grandpa's face turned red. "Carolyn, please stop telling me what to do. I'm perfectly capable of straightening a painting, and I shouldn't have to call on Seth to do every little thing!"

Mother's chin trembled and tears sprang to her eyes. "You

don't have to raise your voice when you speak to me, Papa."

"Sorry," Grandpa mumbled, "but I get tired of you fussing all the time and telling me what to do. I'm not a little boy, and you're not my mother."

"No, I'm a daughter who's concerned about her father's welfare. Is there a law against that?"

"Of course not, but—"

David cleared his throat real loud. "I'd be happy to straighten the picture for you, and then I need to get back to work."

"There's no need for that," Grandpa was quick to say. "I can climb back on the ladder and finish the job I started." His gaze swung to Mother then back to David. "And since your mother's so worried about me, she can hold the ladder to keep it steady."

Mother planted both hands on her hips and scowled at him. "I will not hold the ladder so you can go back up there! We need to wait until Seth gets here so he can do the job we're paying him to do."

Grandpa opened his mouth as if to say more, but then he

clamped it shut and headed for the front door.

"Where are you going?" Mother called to his retreating form.

"Out for a walk. I think a bit of fresh air might do me some good." He glanced over his shoulder at David. "You may as well head back to your shop."

"What about the picture?"

"I've changed my mind. It can wait for Seth."

As Grandpa hurried out the door, David turned to Mother and said, "I hope the rest of your day goes well."

Her forehead creased as she frowned. "I doubt it. When your grandfather returns, he'll probably get involved with something else he shouldn't be doing."

David gave her arm an easy pat and went out the door, smiling to himself. Some things never seemed to change.

❄

"This place is so small," Helen told Elizabeth for the fifth time since they'd begun cleaning the cabin. "I don't see how you're going to live in such cramped quarters."

"We'll be fine. It's just going to be the two of us, so we don't need much room. Besides, we can always add on to the cabin when children come. Even so, I'd hate to change anything that might take away from the quaintness my grandpa created."

Elizabeth picked up a rag and began dusting several pieces of furniture that had been left in the cabin and had belonged to her grandparents. Truthfully she looked forward to living here, away from the noise and hustle-bustle of the city, which seemed to be growing rapidly these days. Even as small as the cabin was, Elizabeth looked around and was almost giddy with excitement, knowing this was going to be her and David's first home, where their life together would soon begin.

"You have no indoor necessary room here, and you'll have to heat water on the stove for washing dishes and bathing." Helen gestured to the floor. "There aren't even any carpets on this drab-looking puncheon floor."

"We'll use the outhouse, just like my parents and grandparents did when they lived here." Elizabeth looked down at the short,

thick planks confined by wooden pins. "I can always put some braided throw rugs on the floor."

Helen shrugged and gave an unladylike grunt. "I've finished washing the windows now. What would you like me to do next?"

Elizabeth was about to suggest that Helen go through some boxes of books they'd found earlier, when a knock sounded on the cabin door.

"I wonder who that could be," Helen said.

Elizabeth smiled. "It might be David. When I spoke to him the other day, he said he hoped to come by after he finished working today."

Helen glanced at the simple wind-up clock on the mantel. "It's only two o'clock. Do you think he'd be done this soon?"

"There's only one way to find out." Elizabeth patted the sides of her hair, smoothed the wrinkles in her dress, and hurried across the room. When she opened the door, she was surprised to see Helen's father, Reverend Warner, standing on the stoop with furrowed brows.

"Is Helen here?" he asked. "She said she might be helping you clean the cabin today."

"Yes, she's here, and we're still cleaning." Elizabeth opened the door wider to bid him enter.

Reverend Warner started toward Helen, and she met him halfway. "Is there something wrong, Father?" she asked with a worried expression.

"I don't believe it's anything serious, but your mother isn't feeling well, and I'd like you to come home. I'm sure she won't be up to fixing supper this evening," he added in a desperate tone.

Helen looked at Elizabeth. "Would you mind if I leave early?"

Elizabeth shook her head. "I'll be fine. You're needed at home more than here right now."

"All right then. I'll return your dress to you soon." Helen wrapped her woolen shawl around her shoulders and followed her father out the door.

As Reverend Warner's buggy wheels rumbled down the dirt

road, Elizabeth returned to the job of cleaning, humming softly to herself, enjoying the quiet cabin.

While she worked, childhood memories flooded her mind. Remembering the warmth Mother had brought to this little cabin, Elizabeth could almost smell the homemade bread baking and loved how the aroma lingered long after the loaves had cooled on the rack. She longed after so many years to bring those moments alive once again in this cozy cabin she would soon call home.

After Elizabeth finished dusting an old desk's surfaces, she opened each drawer and cleaned the crevices. One of the drawers, however, seemed to be stuck.

Determined to get it opened, she grabbed the brass knob and pulled as hard as she could. It finally gave way. Inside she found some old drawings she assumed had been done by either Mother or her sister, Lovina. Then, to Elizabeth's surprise, she discovered a battered-looking leather journal crammed in the very back of the drawer. Curious as to whom it had belonged to, she lifted it

out and opened the cover. Aunt Lovina's name was written there.

Elizabeth smiled. *Mother and her sister grew up in this cabin. Aunt Lovina probably sat right here at this desk to write in her journal.* Elizabeth had never been close to her aunt, who as far as she knew had never married. After Aunt Lovina moved to Easton and opened a boardinghouse, Elizabeth hadn't seen much of her. It had always seemed that her aunt preferred keeping to herself. From the few things Elizabeth remembered her mother saying about Aunt Lovina, she'd concluded that the two sisters had never gotten along very well. The last news anyone in the family had heard about her aunt was that she'd sold the boardinghouse and moved, but no one knew where.

Feeling the need for a break and more than a little curious as to what her aunt's journal might say, Elizabeth fixed herself a cup of tea and took a seat on the deacon's bench near the window, placing the journal in her lap.

The first entry was dated June 10, 1856, and included a note about Lovina's sixteenth birthday that day and how she'd received

the journal from her parents. Lovina hadn't written much on the first page, other than to say she hoped to write her innermost thoughts in this little book.

As Elizabeth flipped through the pages, she was careful. Some seemed a bit brittle, and the musty odor reminded her that the journal was old and had probably been stuck in the desk for quite a while.

Elizabeth read a few more pages, smiling when she came to a journal entry about a mouse that had gotten into the pantry and eaten the cookies Grandma had made, and frowning when she read how Aunt Lovina and Elizabeth's mother, who was two years younger than Lovina, had argued about who would wash and who would dry the dishes. Their mother had stepped in and settled the dispute.

Elizabeth sighed. She wished she'd known her mother's parents, but they'd both died before she was born.

She turned several more pages and continued to read, until she came to an entry dated April 20, 1860. It read:

My sister, Cassandra, is marrying Charles Canning today,
but she's taking a horrible secret with her. Cassandra used to
be courted by Raymond Stinner, but when he dropped her
suddenly and married Carolyn Flannigan, she quickly
turned to Charles and agreed to marry him right away. I
wonder what Charles would say if he knew Cassandra was
pregnant with Raymond's baby.

Elizabeth's mouth went dry as she stared at the journal entry, trying to piece things together. Raymond Stinner was David's father. Until now, Elizabeth had no idea he'd courted her mother, much less that she'd been carrying his baby when she married Father. How shocking to learn such a thing about her own mother, whom she'd always held in such high esteem.

But who is that baby? Elizabeth wondered. Her heart began to race. *Could Mother have had a miscarriage, or do I have a brother or sister I don't know about?*

Anxious to learn more, Elizabeth continued turning the pages

in her aunt's journal, until she found one that read:

Christmas Eve, 1860: Cassandra's baby was born today.
Cassandra had told everyone the child was due in
January, but now she's saying the baby came early. That's
just to protect her reputation, of course. She doesn't want
anyone to know—especially not Charles—that she was
pregnant when they got married. She especially doesn't
want him to know that Raymond Stinner is the father of
her baby. The little girl weighs six pounds and seems to be
quite healthy. Of course the reason for that is because she's
not really premature. Cassandra named her baby,
Elizabeth. I guess you could say the child is Cassandra's
little Christmas secret.

Elizabeth swayed unsteadily as the journal slipped from her fingers and dropped to the floor with a thud. If Raymond Stinner was her real father, that meant she was David's half sister!

Stunned, she thought, *No wonder we both have blond hair and blue eyes.*

When the truth of it all set in, she covered her mouth and choked on a sob. "Oh, dear Lord, how can this be? Why did You allow such a terrible thing to happen? I can never marry David now!"

As Elizabeth stared into space, her mind racing, the only thing she could see was her dream of being David's wife and all the wonderful plans they'd made fading further and further away. In a matter of a few minutes, Elizabeth's world had gone from a future filled with hopes and dreams to an unsettling question: *What now?*

Chapter 3

"I got busy workin' and forgot to ask when you first returned to the shop—is your granddaddy okay?" Gus asked David.

David nodded. "He fell off a ladder but wasn't really hurt. Just got the wind knocked out of him, I guess."

"Glad to hear he's all right."

"Grandpa tries to do too much, and Mother worries too much."

Gus chuckled. "Guess that's what women do—worry about those they love."

"I suppose Elizabeth will worry about me after we're married." David reached into his jacket pocket and pulled out the gold timepiece that had belonged to his father. "Speaking of Elizabeth, I think I'll head over to the cabin now and see how she's doing."

Gus's forehead wrinkled. "I thought you were gonna work in the shop until the end of the day."

"I can't concentrate on work right now, and I'm sure you can manage on your own for a while."

Gus shrugged. "It's your right to do whatever you want, 'cause you're the boss."

David grinned and thumped the man's shoulder. "I'll see you bright and early tomorrow morning."

When David mounted his horse and guided him in the direction of the cabin, he began to whistle. He could hardly wait to see his bride-to-be and tell her once more how much he loved her.

❄

Elizabeth paced between the deacon bench and the fireplace, pondering what she should do about her aunt's journal. She couldn't let David or her father see it. Something like this would bring shame on both of their families. She would need to call off the wedding, of course, and the sooner the better. If she just knew what to say to David. This was the most difficult thing she had ever been faced with.

She glanced at her satchel full of cleaning supplies. She would put the journal in there for now until she was able to dispose of it properly.

A knock sounded on the cabin door, causing Elizabeth to jump.

"Who is it?" she called, wondering if Helen had returned to help her finish cleaning.

"It's me, David."

Elizabeth's heart pounded so hard she feared her chest would explode. She had to let David in but wasn't ready to call

off the wedding or offer an explanation. How could she, when she was still trying to grasp this horrible secret that, less than an hour ago, she hadn't even known existed? She'd have to pretend all was well until she figured out the best way to deal with things.

She whispered a prayer for courage, swiped at the tears on her cheeks, and opened the door. "I—I wasn't sure I'd see you today. I figured you'd be hard at work," she said, unable to make eye contact with David.

He stepped into the room and shut the door. "I said I'd try to come by, remember?"

"Yes, but I. . ." She forced herself to look up at him.

"Is everything all right? Your face looks red, and your eyes are puffy. Have you been crying?" David moved closer and held out his arms. His piercing blue eyes seemed to bore right through her.

Elizabeth wished only to be held in the comfort of his embrace, and have this black cloud of uncertainty go away, but

THE Christmas SECRET—37

she quickly stepped back. "I–I'm fine. Just hot and sweaty from working so hard, and I—I may have rubbed my eyes when I was dusting."

"I'm sorry you had to work so hard. Where's Helen, anyway? I thought she was going to help you clean the cabin today."

"She was here earlier—until her father came by and said her mother wasn't feeling well. Helen left with him."

"I'm sorry to hear her mother's ill. Sure hope it's nothing serious."

"Me, too." Elizabeth shivered and moved to stand in front of the fireplace, feeling the need of its warmth.

David stepped up beside Elizabeth and, turning her to face him, pressed his forehead to hers.

Her throat tightened. *He's my brother. He's my brother*, she reminded herself. "David, I. . ."

He pulled back slightly, and his mustache tickled as he brushed a kiss across her forehead. "It won't be long now, and you'll be my wife. I can hardly wait for Christmas Eve."

Cheeks burning and heart pounding, Elizabeth moved quickly away, busying herself as she began to dust the desk where she'd discovered the journal. She'd already dusted it thoroughly but needed to put some distance between her and David.

"It's obvious that there's still some work to be done here, so what would you like me to do?" David asked.

Silence filled the room. *Go home. Leave me alone so I can think.*

"Elizabeth, did you hear what I said?" David touched her arm.

She turned to face him but fixed her attention on the buttons of his jacket, unable to look at his handsome face. "I–I've developed a headache, and my stomach is upset. I think I'd better go home and lie down. Besides, it's not proper for us to be here alone together without a chaperone."

"You're right, of course." He retrieved her shawl from the back of the wooden bench and placed it around her shoulders. "I'll follow you home to make sure you get there safely."

"There's no need for that. I'll be fine." Elizabeth grabbed her satchel and hurried out the door.

She was about to climb into her buckboard when David called, "I really would prefer to make sure you get home safely."

"If you wish," she mumbled. The headache she'd mentioned was real and had become worse—no doubt from the time she'd spent crying after she'd found Aunt Lovina's journal. If only she hadn't read those horrible things her aunt had written. If she could just turn back the hands of time.

But if I hadn't read the journal I might have married David—my own brother—and then. . .

No longer able to deal with her troubling thoughts, Elizabeth gathered up the reins and got the horse moving. She needed to get home so she could retreat to her bedroom and think things through. She needed to pray about this matter and decide how she should break her engagement to David. The most frigid of winters had never made her feel as cold as she did right now.

Chapter 4

*U*nable to face David, Elizabeth spent the next several days in bed, telling her father and stepmother, Abigail, that she was sick with a stomach virus. Truth be told, her stomach was upset. Food held no appeal, and she'd had to force herself to drink the chamomile tea Abigail had given her. Father had wanted her to see the doctor, but she'd insisted that it was nothing serious and would be fine in a few days.

I can't stay in my room forever, Elizabeth told herself as she climbed out of bed one morning. *I need to break my engagement to David, and I can't put it off any longer. I need to do it today.*

She wrapped the quilt from her bed around her shoulders and plodded across the room to the window. It was a dreary-looking day, full of dark clouds and a blustery wind that caused the branches of the elm tree near the house to brush against her window with an irritating scrape.

Elizabeth shivered and crossed her arms over her chest. It was cold in her room, and she was tempted to crawl back in bed under the warmth of the covers but knew she'd been confined to her room long enough. She'd made a decision before going to sleep last night and needed to follow through with it. She would get dressed, put Aunt Lovina's journal, as well as a few clothes, into a satchel, and go downstairs for a cup of tea and a biscuit. Then she'd head over to the cabin, leave David a note, and stop on her way to the train station to see Helen, whom she'd decided would be her only confidante. She was glad

Father had left on a business trip to New York this morning, and since Abigail had gone shopping, she wouldn't have to tell them face-to-face that she was leaving. She was sure they wouldn't have accepted her explanation and feared she may have broken down and told them the truth.

I must never tell them, Elizabeth told herself. *It would bring humiliation on my family, and the shock might be too much for Father when he found out he's not my real father at all.*

Tears sprang to Elizabeth's eyes. Was it possible that Father already knew? Could Mother have told him that she was carrying another man's child when she married him? Oh, surely not. If Father knew this horrible secret, he'd never let on or treated Elizabeth any differently than he would his own flesh-and-blood child. He'd always been kind, affectionate, and eager to give her whatever she wanted.

If Mother were still alive, I'd go to her and talk about this. But then, Elizabeth thought, *maybe it's good that I'm not able tell her what I read in Aunt Lovina's journal. I'm sure it would be most*

embarrassing for Mother to learn that I'd discovered her Christmas secret.

Elizabeth stood before the oval looking glass and studied her reflection. *Do I look more like Mother or my real father?* Elizabeth had always thought she'd gotten her mother's blond hair and her father's blue eyes, but when Raymond Stinner was alive, he'd had both blond hair and blue eyes. *Just like David,* she reminded herself.

Elizabeth turned away from the mirror. *Oh, David, I know it's wrong to love you as anything more than a brother, but may God forgive me, I can't seem to help myself.* She nearly choked on the sob rising in her throat. *The only way I can possibly deal with this is to put a safe distance between David and me.*

❅

"How's Elizabeth doing?" David asked when Charles Canning entered his buggy shop. "Is she feeling any better?"

Charles, a tall man with thinning brown hair and pale blue eyes, lifted his broad shoulders in a brief shrug. "She was still in

bed when I left home, so I'm not sure how she's feeling this morning."

"I've been worried about her," David said with concern. "I've stopped by your house a couple of times to see how she's doing, but Abigail always says Elizabeth isn't feeling up to company."

Charles nodded. "She's been staying in her room and hasn't taken any of her meals downstairs, although I don't think she's seriously ill."

"When I'm done working for the day, I think I'll stop by there again. I want to be sure she's not any worse." Despite the fact that it had only been a few days since he'd seen Elizabeth, it felt like forever.

"That's a good idea. If she's feeling up to company today, I'm sure she'll be glad to see you."

"So what'd you come by for?" David asked.

"I'm heading out of town on business today, but before I go, I wanted to drop in here and let you know that I need a new

carriage. It'll be a wedding present for you and Elizabeth."

David chuckled. "It's not often that a man gets asked to make his own wedding present."

Charles thumped David's shoulder. "That's true, and I wouldn't be asking, but you're the best at what you do. I don't want my daughter riding in a carriage built by anyone else."

David smiled. "I appreciate that, sir, but to tell you the truth, I was planning to give Elizabeth one of my carriages as a combination birthday and wedding present. It's a secret, though. I want to surprise her with it."

"That's fine. I won't ruin your surprise, and I'm sure I can find some other suitable gift to give you and Elizabeth on your special day." Charles started to walk away but turned back around. "Are you sure you and Elizabeth want to live in that old cabin where my first wife, Cassandra, and I got our start?"

David nodded with certainty. "It's what Elizabeth wants, and I think we'll be very happy living there."

"Elizabeth's mother and I were happy there, too. But I wish she

had lived long enough for me to give her the house she deserved."

"At least Elizabeth and your second wife have been able to enjoy the fruits of your labor."

"True." Charles's forehead creased. "How long do you think it'll be until you're able to have a home built for you and Elizabeth?"

David shrugged. "I don't know. Hopefully, within the next few years."

"Before children come, I hope. That cabin's too small to raise a family in."

"You did it, sir. You raised Elizabeth there, and from what I understand, your first wife's parents raised two daughters there as well."

Charles nodded. "We managed, but it was crowded, so I hope you and Elizabeth are settled into a roomy home in town before any children come along."

"I understood your concern," David said, "but I promise to take good care of your daughter; of that you can be certain."

Chapter 5

When Elizabeth opened the cabin door and stepped inside, a lump rose in her throat. She'd been looking forward to setting up house in this special little cabin where her only memories of her mother remained. This would never be her home now. She'd been eagerly waiting to become David's wife, but that was obviously not meant to be.

Elizabeth sank into the wooden chair in front of the desk and

buried her face in the palms of her hands. She needed to write David a farewell note and get away from here as quickly as possible, but telling him she was leaving was ever so hard.

She opened the desk drawer and took out a piece of paper. Then, struggling not to cry lest she soil the page, she. began writing:

Dear David,

As hard as it is for me to tell you this, I know I must say what's on my heart, and I hope you'll understand. I've come to realize that we're not meant to be together, so I won't be marrying you on Christmas Eve. I'm going away. Please don't try to find me, because I won't change my mind. It's over between us. I pray that God will bring someone else into your life and that you'll find the happiness you deserve.

Fondly,
Elizabeth

Elizabeth folded the note, slipped it into an envelope, and wrote David's name on the outside. Then she placed it on the fireplace mantel next to the set of wooden candlesticks her father had given her mother on their last Christmas together.

Tears blurred Elizabeth's vision as she stared at the envelope. With an ache in her heart she feared would always remain, she slipped quietly out the door. She had one more stop to make before heading to the train station.

❄

"My mother's better now, and it's good to see that you're finally out of bed, too. How are you feeling?" Helen asked when Elizabeth entered the stately house Helen shared with her parents.

"I'm fine physically, but in here, I'll never be the same." Elizabeth touched her chest and drew in a shuddering breath.

Helen led the way to the kitchen. Then she pulled out a chair at the kitchen table and motioned for Elizabeth to sit down. "You look like you've been crying. What's wrong?"

Elizabeth removed her shawl and draped it over the back of the chair. As she sat, she drew in a couple of deep breaths to help steady her nerves. She had to tell someone the truth about why she was leaving. The secret that lay beneath the pages of her aunt's journal was too much to carry alone. "This is so difficult for me to talk about," she said in a whisper. "Are we alone?"

Helen nodded as she took a seat beside Elizabeth. "Mother's visiting my grandparents today, and Father's attending a deacon's meeting at the church."

With a sense of urgency, Elizabeth leaned forward and clasped her friend's hand. "What I'm about to tell you is a secret, and it must remain so—do you understand?"

Helen nodded. "You've told me secrets before, and I've never betrayed your confidence."

"This secret is different than the ones we shared during our growing-up years. If this secret ever got out, it could ruin several people's lives. It's already ruined mine."

Helen's eyebrows drew together. "What are you talking about?"

"It's a horrible secret that could hurt my father, David's mother, and most of all, David." Tears welled in Elizabeth's eyes as she swallowed against the constriction in her throat. "David can never find out. Do you understand?"

"No, I don't understand. What secret could be so horrible that it would ruin four people's lives?"

Elizabeth reached into her satchel and pulled out the journal. "This belonged to my aunt, Lovina Hess. It was stuck in the back of a drawer, inside the desk I was dusting at the cabin the other day."

"Did something your aunt wrote upset you?"

"Yes. It's the most horrible secret I could ever imagine." Elizabeth opened the journal to the entry she'd marked with a slip of paper and handed it to Helen. "Read for yourself."

Helen placed the journal on the table, and as she read, her mouth formed an *O*. "I—I can't believe it! This has to be a mistake."

Elizabeth slowly shook her head. "I wish you were right, but

it's not a mistake. Aunt Lovina would have no reason to lie about something so serious." Elizabeth touched the netting that held her long blond curls at the back of her head. "It's no coincidence that David and I have the same color hair and eyes. You mentioned it yourself the other day. And David's father—my real father—he had blond hair and blue eyes, too."

Helen stared at the journal; then turning her gaze to Elizabeth, she said, "Have you spoken to your aunt about this?"

"No." Elizabeth released a lingering sigh. "I don't even know where Aunt Lovina lives anymore."

"What are you going to do?"

"I've written a note and left it in the cabin for David."

Helen's eyes widened. "Did you tell him the truth?"

"Of course not. Revealing my mother's secret would be too humiliating for David and both of our families. I told him in the note that I can't marry him because I've come to realize we're not meant to be together, and that I'm going away."

Helen handed the journal to Elizabeth. "I feel so terrible for

you. I wish there was something I could do to make your pain go away."

"You can't take away the pain I feel. It's something I'll have to deal with on my own. But there is something you can do."

"What? I'll do anything to help."

Elizabeth returned the journal to her satchel. "You must keep my secret and never tell anyone."

"What if David asks me if I know why you broke your engagement?"

"You mustn't tell him."

"But where will you go?"

"I'd rather not say right now. I'll write to you in a few weeks after I'm settled in. But you have to promise not to tell anyone where I've gone. Is that clear?"

Helen gave a quick nod. "David will be so hurt when he reads your note."

"I know, but not nearly as hurt as he'd be if he learned that the woman he planned to marry is really his half sister."

"I—I see what you mean." Helen dabbed at the tears beneath her eyes. "I can't believe how quickly things have changed. When we were at the cabin, you were so happy and looked forward to your wedding. Now you won't even be here to celebrate your birthday on Christmas Eve with your family and friends."

"It's for the best," Elizabeth murmured. Oh, how she wished this was just a bad dream and she could wake up and everything would be as it once was.

"Have you told your father and Abigail that you're leaving?" Helen asked.

"I left a note for Father on the desk in his study. I'm sure he'll see it when he gets home from his business trip in New York."

"What did you tell him?"

"Pretty much the same thing I told David. I also said I would write and let them know where I was when I felt that I could." Elizabeth dabbed at her own set of tears. "I hope Father and Abigail will understand."

"This is too much to comprehend," Helen said. "I wish I

knew how to pray about it."

"Pray that David will find someone more suitable to be his wife." Elizabeth pushed back her chair and stood. "You and David have always gotten along well enough. Maybe he'll take an interest in you."

Helen gasped. "Oh no, Elizabeth, I. . ."

Elizabeth turned and rushed out the door. Her heart felt as numb as the cold air that hit her face.

Chapter 6

Elizabeth left Helen's house and hurried down the street. She planned to see if Slim Weaver, the man who ran the livery stable, would give her a ride to the train station. She had to get out of town before she ran into someone she knew. As she neared the Old Corner Store on the southwest corner of Center Square, Howard Glenstone stepped out. He wore a dark brown suit with a beige bow tie and looked as dapper as ever with the ends of his

cocoa-colored hair sticking out from under his top hat.

"It's good to see you, Elizabeth." Howard's handlebar mustache twitched rhythmically as he smiled and gave her a nod. "Where might you be headed on this chilly fall day?" A whiff of Howard's bay rum hair tonic wafted up to her nose.

"I'm. . .uh. . .on my way to the livery stable," she mumbled, refusing to meet his gaze.

"I'm heading to my office, but I'd be glad to give you a ride."

"No thanks. The livery's not far, and I can walk." Knowing she had to hurry or she would miss her train, Elizabeth continued walking at a brisk pace.

"What's your business at the livery stable?" Howard asked as he strode along beside her. "Are you in need of a new horse?"

"I'm sorry, Howard, but I'm in a hurry and really can't talk anymore."

"Oh, I see." He gave her a nod and turned toward his exquisite-looking emerald-green carriage with gold mountings. Howard was not only handsome, but he was also a man of wealth

and prestige with many business holdings. He would no doubt make some lucky woman a good husband—just not her. She would forever remain an old maid.

When Elizabeth arrived at the livery stable, she spoke to Slim about giving her a ride to the train station.

"Sure, no problem." Slim offered Elizabeth a toothless grin. "Goin' to Philadelphia to do some shoppin' for your weddin', I'll bet."

Elizabeth made no reply as Slim helped her into the buggy. She didn't feel right about not answering his question, but she couldn't tell him the truth. It wasn't like her to be antisocial. She felt awkward, almost guilty, treating those she'd known since childhood with this silence, but for now, she had no other choice. The fewer questions, the better.

As the horse and buckboard left the livery stable, Elizabeth glanced over her shoulder and caught sight of David's employee, Gus Smith, crossing the street. She wasn't sure if he'd seen her or not but was relieved to see that David wasn't with him. She certainly couldn't deal with seeing him right now.

✳

David urged his horse to move quickly as he headed down the road toward the cabin. He'd stopped by the Cannings' to see Elizabeth, but Abigail, who'd just returned home from shopping, said Elizabeth wasn't there. She thought Elizabeth might have gone to the cabin. But as David approached the cabin, he didn't see any sign of Elizabeth's buckboard. Could she have come on foot? It was worth checking.

David tied his horse to the hitching rail, sprinted to the cabin, and was surprised to find the door ajar. The room was cold, and there was no sign of a fire having been built in the fireplace. He glanced at the mantel and noticed an envelope with his name on it.

He tore it open, and as he read the note, his heart started to pound. *What? Elizabeth isn't going to marry me?* For some reason she thought they couldn't be together. But why? In all the time they'd been courting she'd never given him any indication that she didn't care for him. Until she'd taken ill several days ago,

everything had appeared to be fine. Had she been lying all this time, pretending to love him when she didn't? Could there be another man? But if that were so, why hadn't she told him sooner? Why wait until now. . .less than two months before their wedding? And why had Elizabeth come to the cabin to clean and get it ready for them to move into if she wasn't planning to marry him? None of this made any sense.

The only thing David could think to do was to find Elizabeth and hear from her own lips why she'd written the note that had caused all this doubt to suddenly enter his mind.

He stuffed the note in his jacket pocket and hurried out the door. He had to go back to Elizabeth's house. If she wasn't there, he'd speak to Abigail about the note. It couldn't end like this. He had to find out why Elizabeth had changed her mind about marrying him and win her back.

Chapter 7

As Elizabeth sat on the train heading for Coopersburg, she stared out the window at the passing scenery, feeling as gloomy as the gray sky above.

She was leaving behind the only home she'd ever known. . . and the only man she'd ever loved enough to marry.

"Are you all right, dear?" the elderly woman sitting beside Elizabeth asked.

Using the corner of her handkerchief, Elizabeth dabbed at the tears wetting her cheeks. "It's nothing, really. I'm just feeling a little weepy right now."

The woman nodded. "I understand. We women are sometimes prone to crying, even when there's nothing to cry about."

Elizabeth gave no reply. She certainly had a good reason to cry but wasn't about to tell this stranger her problems. It was bad enough that she'd told Helen the truth. In another time she might have welcomed a conversation with this kindhearted woman, but instead, she leaned her head against the back of the seat and closed her eyes, trying to calm the knot in her stomach. This was certainly not a journey she'd ever imagined taking. *I do hope Helen keeps my secret. Please, Lord, help me not to be afraid, and lead me down the right path in the days ahead.*

❄

As David urged his horse toward Elizabeth's house, his shop came into view. As he approached the building, Gus stepped out

and motioned him to stop.

David halted his horse. "What is it, Gus?"

"I could use your help putting some wheels on that fancy, plum-colored carriage we got in the other day."

"You'll have to manage on your own for a while," David said. "I'm going over to the Cannings' house to talk to Elizabeth right now."

Gus shook his head. "I don't think she's there, boss."

"How do you know?"

"Saw her with Slim Weaver, and it looked like they was headin' toward the train station in his buckboard."

David's heart gave a lurch. Apparently Elizabeth had followed through with her threat to leave town. He certainly hadn't expected her to leave so soon.

David quickly told Gus about the note he'd found in the cabin.

"So she gave ya the mitten, huh?"

"Yes. I'm afraid she has discarded me as her boyfriend,"

David said with regret.

Gus frowned. "Sorry to hear that. Thought you two was madly in love."

"That's what I thought, but I guess I was wrong." Inside, though, David still had a hard time believing it.

"I've got to go now. I need to find out where Elizabeth has gone!" David clutched the reins so tightly that his fingers ached as he clucked to the horse. Hurrying through the streets of town, he nearly collided with one of the elderly street vendors hawking his goods. As he pulled his horse to the right to dodge the vendor's cart, he heard the man's rhythmic chant: "Scissors to grind! Razors. . .scissors. . .penknives to grind!"

David continued on, until he came to the Cannings' large, gingerbread-trimmed home. He secured his horse to the hitching rail, sprinted up the porch steps, and gave the bellpull a yank.

Several minutes later, Abigail answered the door. "May I help you, David?"

"I went to the cabin, hoping Elizabeth was there, but I found this instead." He pulled the envelope from his pocket and handed it to her.

"What is it?"

"A note from Elizabeth. She left it on the fireplace mantel for me."

Abigail slipped the note from the envelope and gasped when she read it. "This is certainly a shock! I had no idea Elizabeth was planning to leave town or that she had decided to break her engagement." She patted her flushed cheeks and pushed a stray tendril of dark hair into the chignon at the back of her head.

"My helper, Gus, said he saw Elizabeth with the man who owns the livery stable and that it looked like they were heading to the train station. Do you have any idea where she might be going?"

Abigail slowly shook her head. "I wonder if Elizabeth left a note for us somewhere in the house. If she did, it might say." She

opened the door wider and bid him in. "If you'd like to take a seat in the parlor, I'll have a look around."

David seated himself on a dark blue, circular sofa, while Abigail hurried off to another room.

Several minutes later she returned, holding an envelope and wearing a glum expression. "I found a note from Elizabeth on Charles's desk in his study."

David leaped to his feet. "What does it say?"

"Pretty much the same as the note she wrote to you—that she's come to realize she can't marry you and has decided to go away. She also said she was sorry that she won't be here for her birthday or Christmas."

"Did she say where she was going?"

"No, and I dread telling Charles when he gets home from his trip. He's going to be very upset."

"He can't be any more upset than I am. Elizabeth was supposed to be my wife." David frowned. "I don't understand what went wrong. One minute she seemed so happy about marrying

me, and the next minute she says she can't marry me at all. It doesn't make a bit of sense."

Abigail sank to the sofa. "Maybe she's not ready for marriage. Maybe she's still too immature and has made herself sick thinking about it."

David flinched. The thought that Elizabeth had made herself sick because she didn't want to get married made him feel guilty. Had he pushed her too hard? Should he have waited another year to propose?

He turned toward the door. "I'd better go. I need to get back to my shop, but before I do, I'm going by Helen's house and see if she knows where Elizabeth went." He hurried out the front door.

❄

A short time later, David entered the Warners' front yard and gave the brass knob a quick pull.

"Is Helen at home?" he asked when Helen's mother, Margaret, answered the door.

"She's in the parlor, practicing the piece she'll be playing for

church this Sunday," the petite woman replied.

"May I speak with her? It's of the utmost importance."

Margaret hesitated a moment and finally motioned to the room on her left. "Go on in."

David stepped into the parlor, where Helen sat in front of a spacious organ, pumping her feet as she played and sang, "Sweet hour of prayer, sweet hour of prayer, that calls me from a world of care, and bids me at my Father's throne, make all my wants and wishes known!"

When David moved closer to the organ, Helen's head jerked, and she blinked several times, looking up at him like a frightened bird. "Oh my! You startled me, David. I—I didn't know anyone had come in."

"I need to speak to you. Your mother said that I could come in."

"Wh—what did you wish to speak with me about?" Helen seemed nervous, which was out of character for this usually calm, confident woman.

He reached into his jacket pocket and pulled out Elizabeth's note. "I found this at the cabin."

Helen dropped her gaze to the organ keys.

"It's a note from Elizabeth."

Still no comment.

Why is she acting so strange? She must know something, and I have to find out what it is.

"She called off our wedding and has gone away," he said.

"I'm very sorry, David."

"Did you know about this?" he asked, taking a seat on the bench beside her.

She nodded slowly.

"Where is she, Helen? What caused Elizabeth to change her mind about marrying me?"

Helen's shoulders trembled as she lifted them in a brief shrug, refusing to make eye contact with him.

David placed his hand on her shoulder. "Please tell me what you know. I can't bear the thought of losing Elizabeth. I love her so much, and until I found this note, I was sure she loved me, too."

Helen's chin quivered as tears gathered in the corners of her chestnut-colored eyes. "I know this is painful for you, David, but you must accept Elizabeth's decision and get on with your life."

"Get on with my life?" He shook his head vigorously. "How can I accept her decision when I don't understand the reason she called off the wedding?"

Helen said nothing.

Irritation welled in David's soul. Helen was hiding something; he was sure of it. Was she trying to spare his feelings, or had she promised Elizabeth not to tell?

"Is there someone else?" he questioned. "Is Elizabeth in love with another man?"

"No."

"Then what is it? Why couldn't she look me in the eye and tell me that she doesn't love me anymore?"

Helen rose from the bench and moved over to the window. "I can't discuss this with you. I gave Elizabeth my word."

"If you won't tell me why she wrote the note and left town, then at least tell me where she's gone," he said, quickly joining her at the window.

"I—I truly don't know." Helen whirled around and dashed out of the room.

David's heart sank. If Helen knew the truth but wouldn't tell him, how was he ever going to get Elizabeth back?

Chapter 8

$\mathcal{E}$lizabeth took a seat in the spindle-backed rocking chair by the fireplace and placed her Bible in her lap. She'd arrived at her grandparents' house in Coopersburg two days ago and had been welcomed with open arms. She was relieved that they'd accepted her excuse for being here and hadn't questioned her about the reason for her breakup with David. All she'd told them was that she'd changed her mind and had come to realize

the two of them weren't meant to be together. Grandma had hugged her and said, "Remember, dear, you're welcome to stay with us for as long as you want."

That could be indefinitely, Elizabeth thought, *because as long as David lives in Allentown, I don't see how I can return. It's hard to think of him as my brother, and I simply can't face him again, knowing the terrible secret that lies between us.*

Forcing her thoughts aside, she opened the Bible. Her gaze came to rest on Proverbs 3:5, a verse she'd underlined some time ago: "Trust in the Lord with all thine heart; and lean not unto thine own understanding."

She was trying to trust God, but it was difficult when her world had been torn apart and there was no hope of her ever marrying David.

Elizabeth heard whispered voices coming from the kitchen, where her grandparents had gone to have a cup of coffee. Her ears perked up when she heard Grandma say, "Elizabeth is so sad. I wish there was something we could do to make her feel better."

"She's obviously hurting over her breakup with David," Grandpa said. "It's going to take her some time to get over it."

I'll never get over it, Elizabeth thought as tears sprang to her eyes. *As long as I live, I'll never forget what David and I once had, and I'll never let myself fall in love with another man.*

Unable to eat, sleep, or work for the past two days, David decided the only thing he could do was to go back to Helen's, hoping he could convince her to tell him something. He needed to know why Elizabeth had broken up with him and where she had gone. He needed to speak with her, and he wouldn't take Helen's no for an answer this time.

When he stepped up to the Warners' front door and rang the bell, Helen answered, wearing an apron splattered with flour over her long, calico dress.

"I need to speak with you. May I please come in?" he asked, praying she wouldn't say no.

She hesitated but finally said, "Father's in the parlor, studying his sermon for this Sunday, and I was in the kitchen making some bread, but I suppose we could speak in there."

"That's fine." David entered the house and followed Helen to the kitchen.

"Would you like a cup of coffee or some tea?" she asked after he'd taken a seat at the table.

He gave a nod. "Coffee sounds good."

She went to the coal-heated stove and picked up the coffeepot.

"Aren't you going to join me?" he asked when she handed him a cup of coffee and moved over to the cupboard next to the stove.

She shook her head. "I have bread dough to knead."

David blew on his coffee then took a sip. The warm liquid felt good as it trickled down his parched throat.

"What did you want to talk to me about?" Helen asked, turning her back to him as she began to work the dough.

"I need to know why Elizabeth left and where she's gone."

Helen whirled around, lifting her flour-covered hands. "I wish you'd stop asking me about this. I promised Elizabeth I

wouldn't say anything about what she'd read in her aunt's journal."
She gasped and covered her mouth with the back of her hand.
"I—I didn't mean to say that. I meant to say. . ."

David leaped to his feet. "What about her aunt's journal?
What's it got to do with Elizabeth leaving?"

Helen sucked in her lower lip as her gaze dropped to the floor.

David clasped her arm. "Please, you've got to tell me. I love
Elizabeth, and I have the right to know why she called off our
wedding."

Helen moaned and flopped into a chair at the table. "I agree,
you do have the right to know, but it's going to come as a shock,
and it's going to hurt you the way it did Elizabeth when she
found out the truth."

"The truth about what?" David took a seat across from Helen
and leaned forward, anxious to hear what she had to say. "What
could Elizabeth's aunt have written that would have caused
Elizabeth to go away?"

David sat in stunned silence as Helen told him about the

entry in the journal.

"So as I'm sure you now realize," Helen said in a tone of regret, "Elizabeth is your half sister, which means you can never be married."

David groaned. This was worse than he could have imagined! No wonder Elizabeth had run away. Learning that she was the illegitimate daughter of David's father had to have been a terrible shock.

"Is Elizabeth sure that what she read is the truth?" he asked, grasping for any ray of hope. "Has she spoken to her aunt about this?"

Helen shook her head. "She doesn't know where her mother's sister is, but I'm sure it has to be true. I mean, why would Elizabeth's aunt write something like that if it wasn't true?"

"What's the aunt's name—do you know?"

"Lovina Hess."

"Where is Elizabeth now?" David asked. "I really must speak to her about this."

"I honestly don't know. I haven't heard anything from her since she left home, and when I spoke to her stepmother the other day, she said she hadn't heard from Elizabeth either."

"Will you let me know if you do hear from her?" he asked as a feeling of desperation gripped him like a vice.

Helen shook her head. "That's not a good idea."

"Why not?"

"It would be too painful for Elizabeth to see you again, and nothing would be gained by hashing this over with her."

Forgetting about the coffee, David rose from his chair. "Thank you for at least telling me about the journal. There's a small measure of comfort in knowing that Elizabeth didn't leave because she's in love with someone else." He turned and walked out the door, a sense of determination welling in his soul. Despite what Helen had said, he would somehow find Elizabeth and try to offer her some comfort. Truth was, he needed comfort right now as well.

Chapter 9

$\mathcal{J}$t had been two weeks since Elizabeth had arrived at her grandparents' house, and with each passing day she became more despondent. Even the delicious Thanksgiving meal Grandma fixed for the three of them yesterday had done nothing to lift Elizabeth's spirits. All she could think about was that Christmas was only a month away and she would not be getting married to the man she loved.

She thought about the telegram her grandparents had received from her father the day he'd returned from his business trip and discovered she was gone. His message said he wondered if she may have come here and that he and Abigail missed her and hoped she would come home soon. Elizabeth had sent a reply, letting him know she was here and missed them, too, but that she planned to stay with Grandpa and Grandma for now. She also asked that he not tell anyone where she was—especially David. Then she'd written a letter to Helen, telling her the same.

Dear Lord, please help me, she prayed. *Take away the ache in my heart and the love I feel for a man I can never marry.*

"You've been sitting in that chair, staring at the fire for hours," Grandpa said, touching Elizabeth's shoulder. "Why don't you put on a wrap and take a ride with me and your grandma? The fresh air might do you some good, and since we'll be stopping at a couple of stores, you can do a bit of Christmas shopping." He chuckled. "Your grandma always says she feels better whenever

she's able to buy anything new—even if it's for someone other than herself."

"You two go ahead," Elizabeth replied. "I'm not in the mood to do any shopping."

"You're not doing yourself any good by sitting here pining every day. If you miss David so much, then you ought to return to Allentown and marry him."

Unbidden tears sprang to her eyes. She wished it were as easy as Grandpa suggested. "I—I can't. It's over between me and David."

"Are you saying you don't love him anymore?"

She shook her head. "We're not meant for each other, and I'm glad I found out before it was too late."

Grandpa's bushy gray eyebrows furrowed. "I'm not sure why you think that, but if you're in love with the young man, that's all that counts. Your grandma and I don't see eye to eye on everything, but our love for each other is what's kept us together all these years." He gave her shoulder a gentle squeeze. "If you and David

had a disagreement, then you ought to resolve it."

She swallowed a couple of times, trying to push down the lump in her throat. "The problem between David and me is not one that can be resolved."

"If you want my advice, the best thing you can do is pray, and ask God to give you some answers."

"I have been praying, but there are no answers for my problem." Unable to talk about it any longer, Elizabeth stood. "I'm tired. I think I'll go upstairs and take a nap." She hurried from the room. There was no way she could explain the situation to Grandpa. It was too humiliating to talk about.

❄

David paced from one end of his shop to the other. In the two weeks since he'd learned why Elizabeth had left town, he hadn't been able to think of much else. He was consumed with the need to speak to Elizabeth's aunt, but no one seemed to know where she was.

His thoughts took him to the day Elizabeth's father had

returned from his business trip in New York. David had gone to the Cannings' house, asking if Charles knew where Elizabeth had gone. Charles said he'd received word from her via a telegram, but that she'd asked him not to tell anyone where she was. Feeling more frustrated than ever, David had then asked Charles if he knew where Elizabeth's aunt, Lovina Hess, lived. Charles had looked at him strangely and asked why he would need to know that. Without revealing what Helen had told him about Lovina's journal, David said he had a question he wanted to ask Lovina about something Elizabeth had found in the cabin. To that, Charles said Lovina had once owned a boarding home in Easton, but after she'd sold it and moved, none of the family had heard from her since.

"I wish Father were still alive so I could ask him about this," David murmured as his mind snapped back to the present. Someone had to know if what Lovina wrote was the truth. Had David's father been aware that Elizabeth's mother had been carrying his child? David knew from what Elizabeth told him

when they'd begun courting that her maternal grandparents were dead, so he couldn't ask them. He also knew that Lovina was Cassandra's only sibling, so Elizabeth had no other aunts or uncles on her mother's side.

"How come you've been pacin' back and forth liked a caged animal for the last fifteen minutes?" Gus asked, stepping up to David with a curious expression.

David stopped pacing. "I'm pondering a problem."

"What kind of problem? Are you havin' trouble with one of the carriages you've been workin' on?"

"No. I've been wondering where Elizabeth's aunt lives."

Gus's forehead wrinkled. "Why would ya be lookin' for Elizabeth's aunt?"

"I need to talk to her about something she wrote in her journal—a journal Elizabeth found in the log cabin that was supposed to be our home after we got married." David frowned. "The problem is, no one seems to know where Lovina Hess lives."

Gus tipped his head. "Lovina Hess, you say?"

"That's right."

"I know of a woman by that name."

David's eyebrows shot up. "You do?"

Gus gave a nod. "Sure thing. My cousin Rosie's a nurse, and she works for a woman named Lovina Hess who has the palsy and a weak heart. Since Miss Hess can't manage on her own anymore, Rosie's been carin' for her these past five years."

For the first time, hope welled in David's soul. "Where does your cousin live?"

"In Philadelphia. 'Course, the woman she works for might not be Elizabeth's aunt."

"Maybe not. It could just be a coincidence that they have the same name, but I need to find out. Do you have the woman's address?"

"Sure do. Got it off the envelope when Rosie wrote to me some time ago." Gus shrugged. "Don't have it with me, though. It's at home in my dresser drawer."

"Would you get it for me?" David asked.

"I'll bring it to work tomorrow mornin'."

"I can't wait that long. I need it right away." David pointed to the door. "I'd like you to go home now and get that address for me."

Gus made a sweeping gesture of the carriage shop. "We've got work to do here. Can't the address wait till mornin'?"

David shook his head. "The work can wait awhile, and I'll pay you for the time it takes to get to and from your house."

Gus pulled his fingers down the side of his bearded face. "If it's that important to ya, then I'll head over there right now." He grabbed his jacket and hurried out the door.

David lifted a silent prayer. *Thank You, Lord.* Now all he had to do was secure a train ticket to Philadelphia. Hopefully, the woman Gus's cousin worked for was indeed Elizabeth's aunt and he'd have the opportunity to speak with her about the journal.

Chapter 10

s David ascended the steps of the two-story wooden-framed house at the address Gus had given him, his heart started to pound. What if the woman who lived here wasn't Elizabeth's aunt? What if she was but wasn't willing to speak with him? If this was the right Lovina Hess, then he couldn't return home without some answers. He simply had to know if what had been written in the journal was true.

Seeing no bellpull, he rapped on the door a few times and waited. Several minutes later the door opened, and a middle-aged woman with mousy brown hair worn in a tight bun greeted him.

"May I help you, sir?"

"Yes. Well, I hope so. I'm told that Lovina Hess lives here."

The woman gave a nod. "That's correct. I'm her housekeeper, Mrs. Cook."

David shuffled his feet a few times. "Uh. . .if it's all right, I'd like to speak with Lovina."

"Please state your name and the nature of your business."

"I'm sorry. I should have told you that right away." David cleared his throat and loosened his shirt collar, which suddenly felt too tight around his neck. "I'm David Stinner. I make and repair carriages in Allentown."

Mrs. Cook's brown eyes narrowed as she shook her head. "Miss Lovina has no interest in having a carriage made. She's ill and hasn't been able to leave the house in some time."

"I'm not here to sell her a carriage. I've come to speak with

Lovina about Elizabeth Canning, whom I believe is her niece."

Mrs. Cook tipped her head and studied David intently. "Miss Lovina has never mentioned a niece, and as I said before, she's ill and isn't up to receiving company right now."

"Please, this is very important, and I promise I won't take up much of her time," he pleaded, in a desperate attempt to make the woman understand.

Mrs. Cook hesitated then finally said, "Very well. I'll see if she's willing to talk to you." She closed the door, leaving David standing on the porch in the cold.

" 'Trust in the Lord with all thine heart; and lean not unto thine own understanding,' " David recited. If ever he needed to trust God, it was now.

Dear Lord, he silently prayed as he paced from one end of the porch to the other, *I hope I haven't come all this way for nothing. I pray that Lovina will speak to me. Help me remember to trust You in all things.*

The front door opened, and David whirled around.

"Lovina will see you, but please don't stay too long. She tires easily these days."

Mrs. Cook held the door open and motioned for David to enter the house. Then she led him up a winding staircase and down a long, dark corridor illuminated by only the small oil lamp she carried. With each step he took, David heard his footsteps echoing on the polished hardwood floor.

As he entered a dimly lit bedroom, a sense of hope welled in his chest. For the first time since this nightmare had begun, he felt closer to finding an answer to the question he sought.

David halted inside the door. A feeling of pity tugged at his heart as he stared at the frail-looking woman lying in the canopied bed across the room. He stood like that for several minutes and then moved slowly toward the foot of the bed. A young woman dressed in a nurse's cap, a long, white skirt, and a striped blouse stood off to one side.

"Is your name Rosie?" he asked.

The nurse nodded. "How'd you know?"

"My employee, Gus Smith, said he was your cousin."

She smiled. "That's right. I wrote to him not long ago."

"May I speak with Lovina alone?" David asked.

Rosie shook her head. "You may say whatever you want, but I shall remain here in the room."

David relented and moved to the right side of the bed, realizing that no matter who else was present, the important thing was having his questions answered.

Lovina, so pale and thin, with straw-colored hair and lifeless brown eyes, looked up at him with a curious expression. "My housekeeper said you know my niece, Elizabeth."

David nodded as excitement coursed through his veins. So this was the right Lovina. "Elizabeth and I were engaged—until she read something in your journal."

Lovina lifted a shaky hand and motioned for him to come near. "I can't hear well and don't know what you said."

David leaned closer; so close he could feel Lovina's warm breath on his face, and repeated what he'd said.

"Journal? What journal?" she rasped.

"Elizabeth found it in an old desk in the cabin where she was born."

Lovina closed her eyes, and for a minute David thought she might have fallen asleep. Slowly she opened them again. "I—I did have a journal once. It was a birthday present from my parents."

"Did you write something in the journal about Elizabeth's mother and my father?"

Lovina blinked. "I don't think I know your father. What's his name?"

"Raymond Stinner."

Lovina's whole body trembled as she gasped and tried to sit up.

Rosie stepped forward and took her hand. "Relax, Miss Lovina. Rest easy against your pillow." She turned to David with a scowl and said, "If she doesn't calm down, I'll have to ask you to leave."

"I'm not trying to upset her," he said. "I just need to know the

truth about what she wrote in the journal."

Rosie glanced at the clock on the dresser across the room. "I'll give you five minutes, but that's all."

David leaned a bit closer to Lovina. "I'm Raymond Stinner's son, David. In your journal you wrote that my father and Elizabeth's mother... Well, you said that Cassandra was pregnant with Raymond's child when she married Charles Canning. Is it true?"

Lovina's pale cheeks flushed slightly, and she averted his gaze.

"Is my father Elizabeth's real father?" he persisted.

Tears welled in Lovina's eyes as she stared at the canopy above her head, seeming to let her memories take her back in time.

David bit his lip while waiting to hear the answer he sought.

After several minutes had passed, Lovina whispered something.

"What was that?"

"I made it all up. I never should have written that in my journal."

A sense of relief swept over David, quickly replaced with a

wave of anger. "But, why? What made you write such a horrible thing if it wasn't true?" he shouted, straightening to his full height.

Lovina whimpered and trembled again.

"Lower your voice," Rosie said, looking sternly at David. "Can't you see how upset she's become?"

"I–I'm sorry." He drew in a deep breath and leaned close to Lovina again. "Please, tell me why you wrote what you did."

Lovina's tears spilled over and trickled onto her cheeks. "I wrote it out of spite and frustration." She sniffed deeply. "I was jealous that my sister had married the only man I'd ever loved."

Stunned by this confession, David drew in a sharp breath. "You. . .you were in love with Charles Canning?"

"Yes, but he only had eyes for Cassandra. My heart was broken when he married her. I—I was angry because they loved each other and I was left out in the cold. . .forever to be an old maid."

"I'm sorry about that, but what does it have to do with

Raymond—my father? Why would you have said that he was the father of Cassandra's baby if he wasn't?"

"Raymond had been courting Cassandra, and just when I thought Charles might ask to court me, he turned to her instead."

"So you wrote that Cassandra was pregnant with my father's child, hoping Charles would read it and refuse to marry her?"

"I didn't think anyone would read my journal. I only put my frustrated thoughts on paper in an effort to alleviate my pain. By pretending in my mind that Cassandra only married Charles because she was desperate and needed a husband, I was able to deal with the disappointment I felt because he didn't choose me." Lovina shook her head slowly, as more tears fell. "I—I truly never intended to hurt anyone."

David stood several seconds, staring down at the pathetic, ailing woman. She'd had her heart broken once, and he didn't think he should break it again by telling her what horrible pain the lie in her journal had caused. If he could find out where

Elizabeth had gone and tell her the truth about the journal, he was sure she would agree to marry him, and everything would be all right. When he returned to Allentown, his first stop would be to see Helen. Maybe by now she would have heard from Elizabeth. If so he hoped to persuade her to tell him where Elizabeth had gone.

❄

Elizabeth sat at the table in Grandma's kitchen with a cup of tea and the letter she'd just received from Helen.

Dear Elizabeth:

It was good to finally hear from you and know that you're safe and living with your grandparents.

I wanted to tell you that David came here a few weeks ago, asking if I knew why you'd called off the wedding and had left town. He looked so sad and kept begging me to tell him something. I made the mistake of mentioning that you'd found your aunt's journal, and then before I realized what I

was saying, I'd told him the whole story.

He was shocked to hear that his father is actually your father, too, and I hardly knew what to say. Then he said he wanted to know where you were, but of course I didn't tell him because at that time I didn't know myself.

If you want my opinion, I think you ought to see David and talk to him about this. You should give him a chance to express his feelings, because I'm sure he's hurting as much as you are.

Please write again soon.

With love and good wishes,
Helen

Tears pricked the back of Elizabeth's eyes, and her hands shook as she quickly jammed the letter into her skirt pocket. She couldn't believe Helen had betrayed her confidence and told David about Aunt Lovina's journal. It was just a matter of time before Helen would tell David where she was, and then he would come here. She couldn't face him—couldn't discuss the horrible truth about who her real father was.

She pushed back her chair and hurried into the parlor, where Grandma and Grandpa sat on the sofa, reading.

"I appreciate you putting me up these last few weeks, but I can't stay here any longer," she said.

Grandma looked up. "Are you going home for Christmas?"

Elizabeth shook her head. "I need to go someplace where I can be alone. I need time to think and work things through."

"Have we been too intrusive?" Grandma questioned, her dark eyes full of obvious concern. "Because if we have, we can certainly keep quiet about things."

Elizabeth shook her head. "It's not that. I just need to be by myself for a while."

"Where will you go?" Grandma asked.

"I—I don't know. Maybe I can stay in one of the boarding homes here in Coopersburg."

"But that would cost money," Grandma said, "and why pay for

a room when you can stay right here?"

"Say, I have an idea," Grandpa spoke up. "Why don't you stay in your cousin Marvin's cabin? He and his wife, Isabelle, are in New Jersey right now, visiting her parents. They won't be back until Christmas, so you'd have two weeks to be alone. Then your grandma and I will join the three of you at the cabin for Christmas dinner."

Elizabeth thought about Grandpa's suggestion and finally nodded. "There's just one thing," she said. "I need you both to promise that you won't tell anyone where I've gone."

Grandma's eyebrows lifted. "Not even your father?"

Elizabeth shook her head.

"I'm sure he and Abigail will want to spend Christmas with you. Do you think it's right not to tell them where you are?" Grandpa asked.

"I wrote them a letter saying I would be spending Christmas with you. Please promise that if David comes here looking for me, you won't tell him where I've gone."

Grandpa looked at Grandma, and when she nodded, he looked at Elizabeth and said, "We won't say a word."

"Thank you." Elizabeth turned toward the stairs. "I'd better go upstairs and pack. I need to leave for the cabin right away."

Chapter 11

As David approached the Warners' house, he quickened his steps. He could hardly wait to tell Helen about his visit with Lovina.

As he stepped onto the porch, the door flew open, and a very surprised-looking Helen stepped out, holding a large red bow and several sprigs of holly. "Oh, you scared me, David! I didn't know anyone was on the porch."

"I just got here."

"Well, if you'll excuse me, I was about to put these decorations on the railing, and then I have some more decorating to do inside." She brushed past him and started down the stairs.

"I need to speak with you," he said, matching her stride.

"I—I really don't have time to talk right now."

"It won't take long, and it's very important."

She halted and turned to face him, lifting her chin a notch. "If this is about Elizabeth, I've already told you more than I should have, and I won't tell you anything else."

"It is about Elizabeth, but I think you need to hear what I have to say." He motioned to the house. "Can we go inside where it's warmer so I can tell you my good news?"

"What's that?"

"I discovered that Elizabeth's aunt Lovina lives in Philadelphia, and I went to see her."

Helen's face blanched. "You went there to ask about the journal, didn't you?"

He nodded. "Can we go inside so I can tell you what she said?"

"Oh, all right." Helen turned, and David followed her up the stairs and into the house, where he was greeted by the pleasant aroma of freshly baked apple pies.

"Let's go in there." Helen motioned to the kitchen. "Mother's in the parlor, visiting with some of her friends from church, and I don't want to disturb them."

David entered the kitchen behind Helen, and after she'd placed her holiday decorations on the counter, they both took seats at the table.

"Tell me what Lovina had to say about the journal," Helen said, slipping her woolen shawl off her shoulders and placing it in her lap.

"She said that what she'd written about my father being Elizabeth's father was a lie," David said. Then he went on to explain the rest of what Lovina had told him.

"Oh my!" Helen drew in a sharp breath and covered her

mouth with the palm of her hand. "Elizabeth needs to know about this."

"Yes, she certainly does. She also needs to see the note Lovina signed, admitting she'd lied, and assuring Elizabeth that Charles Canning is indeed her real father."

Helen's face broke into a wide smile. "That's wonderful, David! Elizabeth will be so relieved to hear this news. I should write to her immediately."

"So you know where she is?" he asked.

Helen's cheeks turned pink as she gave a slow nod. "I got a letter from her a while back."

"And you didn't tell me?" David's voice was edged with the irritation he felt.

"Elizabeth asked me not to tell anyone, and since I'd already broken my promise and told you about the journal, I felt I had to respect her wishes and not tell you where she's been staying."

He leaned forward, resting his elbows on the table. "Things

are different now that we know the truth. I feel it's important that I be the one to tell Elizabeth what her aunt had to say."

"I suppose you're right," Helen said with a nod. "She's been staying at her grandparents' house in Coopersburg."

David snapped his fingers. "Of course! Don't know why I didn't think to look for her there."

"Do you have the address?" Helen asked.

"Yes. I went there with Elizabeth several months ago to tell her grandparents that we were engaged."

"When will you leave?"

"As soon as I can secure a train ticket and line out some jobs for Gus to do while I'm gone." David pushed back his chair and stood. "I'm headed over to the shop right now."

Helen smiled. "May God be with you and grant you a safe trip."

❄

Elizabeth had been staying in her cousin's cabin for two days, and despite her desire to be alone, she was lonely and more depressed than ever. Besides missing the sights and sounds of Christmas, being in her cousin's cabin made her think about David and the little cabin they would have shared if they'd been able to get married. Maybe she'd made a mistake leaving Grandpa and Grandma's. She missed Grandpa's cheerful smile and Grandma's tasty cooking. She missed the times she'd spent with them around the fire each evening. At least in her grandparents' house she'd been surrounded by their happiness, making the days a bit more pleasant.

As hard as Elizabeth tried to fight it, the loneliness became heavier, surrounding her like a burdensome piece of clothing. She shivered and tossed another log onto the fire. *If Grandpa were here, he'd be tending the fire, and Grandma would probably be baking.*

With a sigh she took a seat in the rocking chair and pulled a lightweight quilt across her lap. It was cold outside. She could hear the wind whipping through the trees.

Snow could be coming soon, Elizabeth thought. *I wonder if I*

should go outside and bring in a few more logs for the fire. Looking up, she noticed a ladybug creeping along the wall as though desperately searching for a warm gap to crawl into until spring. She remembered reading that in some countries they believed a ladybug was a sign of good luck, and although she didn't believe in folklore, this one time she wished it were true.

As she stared into the fire, she thought about Aunt Lovina's journal and how on the day her grandparents had gone Christmas shopping she'd tossed it into the fire. As she'd watched the flames consume the journal, it had done nothing to alleviate her pain.

Elizabeth leaned her head back and closed her eyes, feeling drowsy from the heat of the fire. *I'll just sit here and rest awhile before I go out for more logs.*

Sometime later, Elizabeth was roused from her sleep by the whinny of a horse. She leaped to her feet and raced to the window, surprised to see her cousin, Marvin, helping his wife,

Isabelle, down from their carriage. As they walked toward the cabin, Elizabeth opened the door.

"Elizabeth, what are you doing here?" Marvin said, a quizzical expression on his face.

Elizabeth quickly explained, adding that their grandparents had said she would be alone until Marvin and Isabelle returned for Christmas.

"My mother is doing better, and so we decided to come back earlier than planned," Isabelle explained. She smiled up at her handsome, dark-haired husband. "We're looking forward to spending our first Christmas together in this cozy little cabin."

"But if you don't mind sleeping in the loft, you're welcome to stay with us for as long as you want," Marvin quickly added.

Elizabeth glanced out the window. It had begun to snow, and even though she felt like an intruder, she knew she couldn't go anywhere tonight. Besides, where would she go? There was some measure of warmth and solace to be found

living under the same roof with family.

"Very well," she said. "I'll stay through Christmas, but then I'll need to find someplace else to go."

Chapter 12

The following afternoon, Elizabeth stared out the cabin window at the swirling snow. "The weather seems to be getting worse," she said to Marvin, who had just thrown another log on the fire.

He joined her at the window. "I believe you're right, so I think I'd better go outside and cut some more wood. We don't want to run out."

"That's a good idea," Isabelle spoke up from her chair across the room, where she sat with some mending in her lap. She blinked her hazel-colored eyes and shivered. "If this weather keeps up, it may be hard to find the woodpile, not to mention that it's awfully cold outside."

Marvin nodded. "I'll get my jacket and head out right now."

"Would you like to sit here by the fire with me?" Isabelle asked Elizabeth after Marvin left. "Or should we go to the kitchen and bake some gingerbread?"

"Gingerbread sounds nice." Elizabeth didn't really feel like doing any baking, but if she kept busy, it might take her mind off the fact that she wouldn't be spending Christmas with David, let alone their whole lives together. She couldn't allow herself to think too hard about how her dreams had been shattered, for fear that she would fall into a black hole of despair and never find her way out.

❄

When David stepped off the train, a blast of cold air hit him

full in the face. It had been snowing hard for the last several hours, and the ground was covered with a heavy blanket of white.

Clutching the satchel he'd brought with Lovina's signed confession, as well as the velveteen pouch she'd given him, he trudged toward the livery stable to rent a horse. He hoped the snow didn't get any worse, or he might not be able to see well enough to find his way to the home of Elizabeth's grandparents, on the other side of town.

When David arrived at the Cannings' door sometime later, he was greeted by Elizabeth's grandmother, Mary. "Is Elizabeth here?" he asked. "I need to speak with her."

Mary shook her head. "Elizabeth was here, but she left a few days ago."

"Where'd she go?"

"I really can't say. She asked us not to tell anyone."

David's heart nearly plummeted to his toes. If Mary wouldn't tell him where Elizabeth was, he wouldn't be able to tell her what he'd found out from Lovina.

"I need to speak with Elizabeth," he said. "It's quite urgent."

"My husband and I will be seeing Elizabeth on Christmas, so if you have a message for her, I'll pass it along."

He shook his head determinedly. "I need to tell her myself."

"I don't think so," Mary's husband, Joe, said, stepping up to the door. "Elizabeth obviously doesn't want to talk to you, or she wouldn't have called off the wedding and left home."

David winced, feeling as if he'd been slapped. He didn't need the reminder that the woman he loved had run away without even telling him why.

"There is something Elizabeth doesn't know, and if I could just have the chance to explain. . ."

"Why don't you come inside? You can explain it to us, and then we'll decide," Mary said. She opened the door wider, and David followed her and Joe into the parlor. He spent the next several minutes telling them about Lovina's journal and ended by saying that the lie Elizabeth's aunt had written was the reason

Elizabeth broke up with him and came here.

Mary gasped, and Joe's handlebar mustache twitched up and down.

"Elizabeth needs to know the truth about this," Joe said.

"Will you tell me where she is?" David asked, fighting his impatience.

"Elizabeth's staying at a cabin outside of town," Joe replied. "You'll need to go out the main road and follow it north about a mile or so, and then turn left at the fork in the road. The cabin is about a mile down from there."

"Since it's snowing so hard, and it'll be dark soon, you might get lost," Mary said with a look of concern. "Why don't you spend the night here and start out fresh in the morning?"

David shook his head. "Elizabeth and I have been apart too long already, so I'll head for the cabin right now." He bid Mary and Joe good-bye and hurried out the door.

As David headed down the road on the horse he'd rented, his hopes soared. Soon he'd see Elizabeth, and once he'd shown her

Lovina's confession, everything would be all right. While he continued on, he allowed the winter scene before him to renew his Christmas spirit. There was something magical about the snow when it came before the holiday. It had a way of bringing out that little-boy feeling he remembered so well in anticipation of a white Christmas.

David's spirits rose a little more, hoping this Christmas would turn out to be all that he and Elizabeth had looked forward to before she'd found the journal.

When he came to the fork in the road that Joe had mentioned, he guided the horse to the left. He'd only gone a short ways when the wind picked up, and the snow came down with such thick flakes that he could barely see. He was quickly losing the light of day, and the horse wasn't cooperating at all. The mare tossed her head from side to side, reared up a couple of times, and finally refused to go.

With a disgruntled groan, David climbed down. He was about to grab the horse's reins when it bolted and ran,

knocking him to his knees. As he attempted to get up, his foot slipped on an icy patch of snow. *Crack!* Instant fear gripped him like a vise, and before he could take any action, he fell through the thin ice into a pond that had been obscured by all the snow.

Chapter 13

As David thrashed about, trying to stay afloat, the ice-cold water stung his entire body like needles. He struggled to breathe in.

Think, David. Think. Don't panic.

He looked around frantically, searching for anything he might use to pull himself out. Nothing. Nothing at all.

Think. Pray. Get your thoughts together, and do what you can to

get yourself out of here.

Instinctively, David began to bob up and down like a cork. This helped to get his chest and belly high enough so he could eventually fall over on top of the ice. Crawling carefully and quickly to the safety of a snowbank, he stood on shaky legs that were fast growing numb. He paused to thank God that he was safe and unharmed, although thoroughly drenched and shivering badly from the frigid water.

A whinny alerted him that his horse was nearby, and relief rushed through him when he spotted the mare standing beneath some nearby trees.

Grunting, he climbed onto the horse's back and gathered up the reins, thankful that the horse didn't spook. His hands were totally numb, and it was hard holding on to the reins with stiff, ice-covered gloves. David had only two choices. He could either turn around and head back to town or keep going, hoping the cabin where Elizabeth was staying wasn't far from here. The faint smell of woodsmoke in the air was a good sign that he might be closer than he thought.

With faith driving him forward, David urged the horse on until he noticed a flicker of light in the distance. Determination to see Elizabeth gave him the burst of energy he needed to keep going.

A short time later he spotted the cabin; a lantern glowed in the window. As he guided the horse to the hitching rail, he saw Elizabeth with her back facing the window. As he removed his satchel from the saddle horn and climbed down from the horse, his heart skipped a beat at the mere sight of her. Just a few steps and he'd be at the cabin, where warmth and protection from the cold beckoned him. More importantly, he could tell Elizabeth that the dreams they once had were not dead, but very much alive. He was almost to the door when he saw a young man with dark, curly hair step up to Elizabeth and give her a hug.

David's heart sank all the way to his freezing toes. He was too late—Elizabeth had found someone else. He turned toward his

horse, ready to admit defeat, but the numbing cold in his limbs won out. He had to get inside where it was warm, or he would surely freeze to death.

With a trembling hand and an ache in his heart worse than the ache in his body from the frigid weather, he rapped on the door.

❄

When a knock sounded on the cabin door, Elizabeth jumped. Who would be calling at this time of day—especially with the weather being so bad?

"I'll see to it," Marvin said, moving toward the door.

Elizabeth stood off to one side, curious to see who it was. When a man stepped inside, wet and shivering badly, she gasped. "David! What are you doing here?"

"I—I came to t–talk to you about y–your aunt's journal." His teeth chattered so badly he could barely talk. "B–but it appears that I'm t–too late."

Elizabeth nodded slowly. "If you know about the journal, then

you know that it's too late for us. We can never be married."

He shook his head. "I'm not t–talking about that. I'm talking about h–him." He motioned to Marvin. "I saw him h–hugging you in the w–window. Is he your h–husband, Elizabeth?"

"Certainly not. Marvin's my cousin, and this cabin belongs to him and his wife." She motioned to Isabelle, who had just poked her pretty auburn head out of the kitchen.

Wearing a look of relief, David took a step forward, stumbled, and dropped the leather satchel he'd been carrying.

"Whoa!" Marvin reached out and caught David's arm and led him toward the fireplace. "What happened to you? You're sopping wet and covered with ice and snow."

David explained about his accident.

"The first thing we need to do is get you out of those wet clothes." Marvin pointed to the bedroom near the back of the cabin. "If you'll come with me, you can change into one of my woolen shirts and a pair of trousers."

"B–but I need to speak with Elizabeth."

"First things first." Marvin led the way to the bedroom, and David followed.

Elizabeth flopped into the rocking chair and closed her eyes in defeat. Her grandparents had obviously told David where she was. Apparently she couldn't trust anyone.

David and Marvin returned a short time later, and then Marvin suggested that he and Isabelle go to the kitchen so Elizabeth and David could talk privately.

David pulled a straight-backed chair close to the fire and took a seat. Then he turned to Elizabeth, took her hand in his, and said, "I have some good news."

"Wh–what's that?" she asked, barely able to look at him, fearful that she'd give in to her threatening tears.

"We're not related. Your father is Charles Canning, and my father is Raymond Stinner."

"But my aunt Lovina said in her journal—"

"I know what she said." David gave Elizabeth a heart-melting smile. "I found out that Lovina lives in Philadelphia,

and I went there to see her."

"You did?"

He nodded. "Lovina lied. She made the whole thing up because she was in love with Charles Canning, and when he chose your mother instead of her, she was angry and jealous, so she wrote that horrible lie in her journal." David rose from his chair and picked up the satchel he'd dropped on the floor when he'd first come in. He returned to his chair and pulled out a piece of paper. "This is a signed confession from Lovina. She feels horrible about what she wrote and asked me to give you this."

Tears welled in Elizabeth's eyes as she read her aunt's letter of apology, knowing how hard it must have been for her to relive that heartache and admit her mistake. "Oh David, this is a Christmas miracle." Closing her eyes, she silently thanked God for this unexpected turn of events. Instead of being angry with Aunt Lovina, Elizabeth was overwhelmed with appreciation for her aunt's admission to the lie she'd written so long ago.

"You're right—it is a Christmas miracle. It's also an answer to my prayers." David reached into the satchel again and handed Elizabeth a small velveteen pouch.

"What's this?"

"It used to belong to your mother, and your aunt wanted you to have it."

Elizabeth inhaled sharply as she removed a small gold locket from the pouch. "Oh, it's so beautiful."

David stood and gently pulled Elizabeth to her feet. "Elizabeth Canning, will you marry me on Christmas Eve?"

"Oh yes," she said, nearly choking on a sob. "I thank God we're together again, and from now on, there will be no more secrets between us."

Epilogue

On Christmas Eve, snowflakes fell gently outside the window as Elizabeth and David stood in front of the glowing fire inside the small cabin that would soon be their new home. After the blizzard-like weather had abated, they'd left Coopersburg and returned to Allentown to prepare the cabin for their wedding, which was where they'd both wanted to hold the ceremony. David's mother and grandfather, Elizabeth's father and

stepmother, and her grandparents and a few close friends, including Helen and her parents, had come here to witness their marriage.

Elizabeth, wearing her mother's ivory-colored wedding gown and gold locket, had never felt more beautiful. *Oh, how I wish Mother could be here to see me get married.*

"And so," Reverend Warner said, pulling Elizabeth's thoughts aside, "what God has joined together, let no man put asunder." He nodded at David. "You may now kiss your bride."

David lowered his head and gave Elizabeth a kiss so sweet she thought she might swoon.

"Happy birthday, Mrs. Stinner. I have a surprise for you," he whispered when the kiss ended and they'd received congratulations from their family and friends.

"What is it?" she asked breathlessly.

His lips curved into a sly smile. "It's a secret. A Christmas secret."

"I thought there would be no more secrets between us."

"This is a good secret." He slipped Elizabeth's shawl over her shoulders and took her hand. "Come with me, and you'll see what it is."

Leaving the warmth of the cabin, David led Elizabeth out the door, where he motioned to the most elegant-looking, mahogany-colored carriage with brass mountings. It was fit for a princess going to a ball.

"I may not be able to give you a beautiful home just yet," David said, "but at least you'll have a handsome carriage to ride in."

Tears welled in her eyes. "I really don't need a beautiful home or a handsome carriage, but I thank you for such a lovely gift." She leaned her head on his shoulder and sighed. "I found all I'll ever need the day I met you, and I'm perfectly happy to live in our little log cabin for as long as necessary." Just minutes after being pronounced husband and wife, Elizabeth didn't think her heart could be any fuller.

David bent down to give her another kiss, this one even sweeter than the last. As they walked hand in hand back inside

to their family and friends, a tiny movement caught Elizabeth's eye. She smiled to herself when she spied a ladybug crawling on the wall above the mantel.

Elizabeth was sure that God must be looking down from heaven to bless their marriage. "Maybe someday our own son or daughter will begin their life in this log cabin," she murmured against David's ear. A feeling of contentment enveloped her, and she knew without any doubt that this night was just the beginning of many dreams to come true.

Gingerbread

1/2 cup brown sugar
1/2 cup butter
1 egg
1 cup molasses
2 1/2 cups flour
1 1/2 teaspoons baking soda

1/2 teaspoon salt
1 teaspoon ground cinnamon
1 1/2 teaspoons ground ginger
1/2 teaspoon ground cloves
1 cup hot water

In a large bowl, cream together sugar and butter; beat in egg, add molasses. In a separate bowl, sift together the flour, baking soda, salt, cinnamon, ginger, and cloves. Blend into the creamed mixture. Stir in the hot water. Pour into a greased and floured 9-inch pan. Bake 1 hour at 350 degrees.

Grandma's Bread

1/2 cup wild yeast starter
    (stir before measuring)
2 1/2 cups lukewarm water

2 teaspoons salt
1 tablespoon melted butter
5 to 6 cups whole wheat flour

Combine starter, water, salt, and butter; mix well. Slowly stir in 5 cups flour. Continue to add up to a cup of flour until dough starts to ball together. Wet a flat board and your hands. Turn dough out onto surface and knead for 10 to 15 minutes, until the texture of the dough is uniform. Grease a large bowl and place dough inside; cover. Set for 8 to 12 hours. Turn dough out onto a damp surface, and shape into 2 loaves. Place in greased pans and let rise for 2 hours, until doubled in size. Bake at 375 degrees for 30 minutes.

Brown Sugar Pudding

1/2 cup sugar
2 tablespoons butter
1 cup milk
1 cup flour
2 teaspoons baking powder
1/2 teaspoon salt

1/2 cup raisins
1/2 cup chopped walnuts
2 cups water
1 cup brown sugar
2 teaspoons butter
1 tablespoon cornstarch

Cream together sugar and butter; add milk, flour, baking powder, and salt, mixing well. Fold in raisins and nuts. In a saucepan, bring water, brown sugar, butter, and cornstarch to a boil. Boil for 5 minutes. Pour syrup in bottom of baking dish. Top with batter. Bake at 350 degrees for 1 hour.

Wanda E. Brunstetter

New York Times, award-winning author, Wanda E. Brunstetter is one of the founders of the Amish fiction genre. Wanda's ancestors were part of the Anabaptist faith, and her novels are based on personal research intended to accurately portray the Amish way of life. Her books are well-read and trusted by many Amish, who credit her for giving readers a deeper understanding of the people and their customs. When Wanda visits her Amish friends, she finds herself drawn to their peaceful lifestyle, sincerity, and close family ties.

Wanda enjoys photography, ventriloquism, gardening, bird-watching, beachcombing, and spending time with her family. She and her husband, Richard, have been blessed with two grown children, six grandchildren, and two great-grandchildren.

To learn more about Wanda, visit her website at www.wandabrunstetter.com.

Let's Keep In Touch!

Want to know what Wanda's up to and be the first to hear about new releases, specials, the latest news, and more? Like Wanda on Facebook!

 Visit facebook.com/WandaBrunstetterFans

OTHER BOOKS BY
WANDA E. BRUNSTETTER

Adult Fiction

The Prairie State Friends Series
The Decision
The Gift
The Restoration

The Half-Stitched Amish Quilting Club
The Tattered Quilt
The Healing Quilt

The Discovery Saga
Goodbye to Yesterday
The Silence of Winter
The Hope of Spring
The Pieces of Summer
A Revelation in Autumn
A Vow for Always

Kentucky Brothers Series
The Journey
The Healing
The Struggle

Brides of Lehigh Canal Series
Kelly's Chance
Betsy's Return
Sarah's Choice

Indiana Cousins Series
A Cousin's Promise
A Cousin's Prayer
A Cousin's Challenge

Sisters of Holmes County Series
A Sister's Secret
A Sister's Test
A Sister's Hope

Brides of Webster County Series
Going Home
Dear to Me
On Her Own
Allison's Journey

Daughters of Lancaster County Series
The Storekeeper's Daughter
The Quilter's Daughter
The Bishop's Daughter

Brides of Lancaster County Series
A Merry Heart
Looking for a Miracle
Plain and Fancy
The Hope Chest

The Lopsided Christmas Cake (with Jean
Brunstetter)
Amish White Christmas Pie
Lydia's Charm
Love Finds a Home
Love Finds a Way
Woman of Courage

The Amish Millionaire Series
The English Son
The Stubborn Father
The Betrayed Fiancée
The Missing Will
The Divided Family
The Selfless Act